Chocolate Fever

YEARLING BOOKS/YOUNG YEARLINGS/YEARLING CLASSICS are designed especially to entertain and enlighten young people. Patricia Reilly Giff, consultant to this series, received the bachelor's degree from Marymount College. She holds the master's degree in history from St. John's University, and a Professional Diploma in Reading from Hofstra University. She was a teacher and reading consultant for many years, and is the author of numerous books for young readers.

For a complete listing of all Yearling titles, write to
Dell Readers Service, P.O. Box 1045,
South Holland, IL 60473.

**Illustrated by
Gioia Fiammenghi**

A YEARLING BOOK

Robert Kimmel Smith

Chocolate Fever

Published by
Dell Yearling
an imprint of
Random House Children's Books
a division of Random House, Inc.
1540 Broadway
New York, New York 10036

Visit us on the Web! www.randomhouse.com/kids

**Educators and librarians, for a variety of teaching tools,
visit us at www.randomhouse.com/teachers**

ISBN: 0-375-80676-8

Reprinted by arrangement with Coward, McCann, and
Geoghegan, Inc.

Printed in the United States of America

May 2000

10   9   8   7   6   5   4   3   2   1

OPM

*For Heidi and Roger
and all the other
chocolate lovers in the world . . .
especially Alex and Nate!*

Contents

About the Book

HENRY GREEN WAS A BOY who loved chocolate. He liked it bitter, sweet, dark, light, and daily; for breakfast, lunch, dinner, and snacks; in cakes, candy bars, milk, and in every other conceivable form. Henry probably loved chocolate more than any boy in the history of the world.

One day—a day that started off like any other day—Henry found that strange things were happening to him. He made medical history with the only case of Chocolate Fever ever. And then he found himself caught up in a wild, hilarious chase, climaxed by a most unusual hijacking!

Henry's wacky adventures will keep readers laughing out loud, and Gioia Fiammenghi's comical drawings add to the fun.

Chapter 1

Meet Henry Green

THERE ARE SOME PEOPLE who say that Henry Green wasn't really born, but was hatched, fully grown, from a chocolate bean.

Can you believe that?

Anyway, this particular Henry Green we are speaking of *was* really born—not hatched—and had a wonderful mom and dad in the bargain. His father was tall and lean and wore eyeglasses, except when he was sleeping or in the shower. Mama Green, whose name was Enid, was a short, slim woman with blue-gray eyes and a tiny mouth

that always seemed to be on the verge of a smile.

They all lived in an apartment in the middle of the city, along with Henry's older brother and sister. Mark Green was ten and tall and very good to Henry. Except when they would argue, which was often, and then he would hit Henry on the head with anything that was handy, which sometimes was hard. But mostly Mark was fun to be with and only got angry when Henry called him Marco Polo. Mark didn't like that, and who could blame him?

Henry's sister was very, very old. Almost fourteen. She didn't ever argue with Henry or Mark. In fact, she hardly talked to them at all because she was so old and wise and almost grown up. Her name was Elizabeth.

The other morning, which was a schoolday at the end of the week called Friday, Henry, Mark, and Elizabeth were at the table in the dining room having breakfast. Mark was eating fried eggs. Elizabeth was quietly chewing on her usual breakfast of buttery toast and milk. And Henry was midway through his usual breakfast, too. Chocolate cake, a bowl of cocoa-crispy cereal and milk (with chocolate syrup in the milk to make it more chocolatey), washed down by a big glass of chocolate milk and five or six chocolate cookies. Sometimes, when it was left over from the night before, Henry would have chocolate pudding, too. And on Sunday mornings he usually had chocolate ice cream.

The truth was that Henry was in love with chocolate. And chocolate seemed to love him.

It didn't make him fat. (He was a little on the thin side, in fact.)

It didn't hurt his teeth. (He'd never had a cavity in his life.)

It didn't stunt his growth. (He was just about average height, perhaps even a little tall for his age.)

It didn't harm his skin, which had always been clear and fair.

But most of all, it never, never gave him a bellyache.

And so his parents, perhaps being not as wise as they were kind, let Henry have as much chocolate as he liked.

Can you imagine a boy having a chocolate-bar sandwich as an after-school snack? Well, Henry did, just about every day. And when he ate mashed potatoes, just a few drops of chocolate syrup swished through seemed to make them taste a lot better. Chocolate sprinkles sprinkled on top of plain buttered noodles were tasty, too. Not to mention a light dusting of cocoa on things like canned peaches, pears, and applesauce.

In the Greens' kitchen pantry there was always a giant supply of chocolate cookies, chocolate cakes, chocolate pies, and chocolate candies of every kind. There was ice cream, too. Chocolate, of course, and chocolate nut, chocolate fudge, chocolate marshmallow, chocolate swirl, and especially chocolate almond crunch. And all of it was just for Henry.

If there was one thing you could say about Henry it was that he surely did love chocolate. "Probably more than any boy in the history of the world," his mother said.

"How does Henry like his chocolate?" Daddy Green would sometimes joke.

"Why, he likes it bitter, sweet, light, dark, and daily."

And it was true. Up until the day we're talking about right now.

Chapter 2

A Strange Feeling

"BETTER HURRY, KIDS," Mama Green called from the kitchen, "it's almost eight thirty."

"Let's go, slowpoke," Mark said to Henry, "we don't want to be late."

"Just one more chocolate cookie," said Henry. He popped it into his mouth and, still chewing, went to his room to get his books. On the way to the front door Henry went through the kitchen and gathered a handful of chocolate kisses to put into his pocket. He liked to have them handy to munch on at school. But this morning, because he still felt somewhat hungry, Henry stripped the silver wrapping from two kisses and popped them into his mouth. Then, after a quick kiss for Mama Green—a kiss that left a little bit of chocolate on her face—Henry, Elizabeth, and Mark headed out the door on the way to school.

At the corner, Henry and Mark waved good-bye to their sister, who had to take a bus to get to her high school. The boys' school, P.S. 123, was just another block away. At the next corner Mrs. Macintosh, the crossing guard, waved them across the street. "The light is always green for the Greens," she said. It was her own little joke. And she said it just about every morning. This morning only Mark, who was extremely polite, smiled. Henry just didn't feel like smiling. In fact, he was beginning to feel a little strange.

In the schoolyard the boys went separate ways to join their classes. As usual, there was a lot of pushing and shoving and fooling around. But Henry, who was always very good at things like knocking hats off boys' heads and making goofy faces at the girls, was quiet. He didn't even say "hi" when Michael Burke, his best friend, came along. "Well what's the matter with you?" asked Michael, grinning.

"What do you mean, 'what's the matter?'" Henry said. "Can't I just stand here? Do I have to carry on and behave like a nut?"

"OK, OK," said Michael. "You don't have to bite my head off. It's just that you're kind of different today. Not like you at all."

Just then the whistle blew, and all the children began marching into the school building. "I feel funny today," Henry said to Michael. "I have the feeling something's going to happen, and I don't know what."

That exact feeling, that something was going to happen, stayed with Henry all morning. He felt strange in his homeroom, strange when he went to gym class, and in Mrs. Kimmelfarber's math class, he felt strange all over.

Henry couldn't concentrate on what Mrs. Kimmelfarber was saying. He just sort of sat there and stared. Without thinking about it, he was looking at his arm and the back of his hand. And

21

then he noticed something. There were little brown freckles all over his skin. Now this would not have been such a startling discovery except for one thing—those little brown freckles were not there when he woke up this morning!

At the front of the room, Mrs. Kimmelfarber was going through the drill on fractions. She was

saying, "And if I take six and a half and subtract one and a quarter, what will I have left?" She looked directly at Henry, who was looking directly at his arm. "Henry," she asked, "what will I have left?"

"Little brown spots all over," said Henry.

Chapter 3

Mrs. Kimmelfarber's Problem

THERE WAS SILENCE in the room for about two seconds. Then there was a riot. All the girls began to giggle. The boys chortled and chuckled and laughed right out loud. Henry turned red, and Mrs. Kimmelfarber, who did not appreciate the humor of it all, turned white.

She rapped her ruler against the desk and shouted for silence. "Henry Green," she said, "what is the meaning—"

"Little brown spots all over," said Henry. "I was looking at my arm and I have these—"

"Little brown spots all over," interrupted Mrs. Kimmelfarber. "I heard you quite clearly."

"But you see, Mrs. Kimmelfarber, I didn't have them all my life. I didn't even have them this morning. But now—"

"I know." Mrs. Kimmelfarber sighed. "Now you have them all over. I'd better have a look at them." Taking Henry's arm, she led him to the window. "Hmmmm," she said as she peered at his arm, "looks like freckles to me."

"No, ma'am," said Henry. "It just can't be."

"Why not?" said Mrs. Kimmelfarber.

"Because I have clear and delicate skin, like my mother."

"Is that so?" Mrs. Kimmelfarber said. "And who told you that, pray tell?"

"My father."

"Ah," said Mrs. Kimmelfarber, "exactly. Now you are sure you didn't observe this phenomenon before this morning?"

"If that means did I see them," said Henry, "no, I didn't."

"Well, then," she said, "you, Henry Green, stand right where you are. And class," she said, turning to face the room, "you will continue to look at your books until I return. In perfect si-

25

lence," she added as she went out into the hall.

Henry stood, as told, while the class looked at him. Mrs. Kimmelfarber walked the few steps down the hall to Mr. Pangalos' room. She looked through the doorway and waited until Mr. Pangalos glanced in her direction. Catching his eye, she waved him out into the hallway.

"Listen, Phil," she began earnestly, "I want you to take a look at a kid—"

"For heaven's sake, Dolores," said Mr. Pangalos, "I'm right in the middle of Americus Vespucci!"

"Who has little brown spots all over his arms."

"Little brown spots? You got me out here for little brown spots?"

"I thought, maybe, measles?"

"Oh, no," said Mr. Pangalos.

"Chicken pox?"

"Hmm," said Mr. Pangalos. "I'd better take a look."

The two of them turned Henry to the light near the window, right in the corner where the potted plants were growing on the window ledge. Mr. Pangalos poked and prodded and even took

his eyeglasses out of his pocket and put them on. "Freckles," he said finally. "Just freckles."

"Are you sure?"

Mr. Pangalos' round nose twitched, and he sniffed the air. "Chocolate?" he said. "Have they brought the chocolate milk upstairs already?"

"Forget the milk," she cried. "Look! Now he has them on his *face*!"

"Oh, no!" said Henry.

"Oh, yes!" said Mrs. Kimmelfarber.

"Oh, my," said Mr. Pangalos. "And they weren't there before?"

"No. Two minutes ago that boy's face was as clear as day. And now. . . ."

Henry felt as if his heart were about to drop into his shoes. He swallowed hard and stared at the two teachers, who were staring at his face.

"Little brown spots all over," said Mrs. Kimmelfarber. "And I see more of them coming out even as we speak."

A tear, just one, welled up in Henry's right eye and began to trickle down his cheek, running slowly in and out of the little brown spots.

Chapter 4

Pop!

DIRT BREEDS GERMS, Nurse Molly Farthing would often say, and germs have a nasty way of making healthy people ill. Naturally, the infirmary of P.S. 123 was always spotless because Nurse Molly Farthing wouldn't have it any other way. And naturally, as Mrs. Kimmelfarber and Henry rushed through the door that morning, she made both of them go back and wipe their feet on the mat. "And don't bring any of your cocoa in here," Nurse Farthing added. She sniffed the air loudly.

"Cocoa?" said Mrs. Kimmelfarber.

"Don't think I don't smell it," Nurse Farthing said.

"Please, Nurse Farthing," said Mrs. Kimmelfarber, "we have an emergency on our hands. This is Henry Green. He's breaking out in a rash of some sort."

"So I see," said Nurse Farthing. She sat Henry down in a chair and turned on a bright light. Pushing her spectacles down to the tip of her nose, she bent close to Henry and looked him over. "It's a rash all right," she said at last. "Peculiar. Looks like little brown spots all over."

"Exactly," Mrs. Kimmelfarber said. "But what is it?"

"Have you ever had measles?" Nurse Farthing asked.

"Yes," said Henry, "when I was five."

"Chicken pox?"

"When I was three and a half."

"Then I would say you have an unidentified rash. And frankly, I don't like the look of it."

Henry, who up until now was merely frightened, began to feel terrified. Nurse Farthing laid her cool hand on his arm and steadied him. "There, there, dear," she said. "Nothing to be frightened of. I'm sure it's not serious. How do you feel?"

"Not very good," said Henry.

"Warm?"

"No."

"Cold?"

"No."

"Dizzy?"

"No," said Henry. "I just feel . . . strange."

"You poor dear," said Nurse Molly Farthing, "you really must be frightened." She ran her fingers through his hair and patted the back of Henry's neck. Somehow this made him feel a little better.

Pop!

"Did you say something?" asked Nurse Farthing.

"No, ma'am," said Henry.

Pop!

"What is that noise, then?" she asked. "It sounds like something going pop."

31

"I heard it, too," said Henry.

"So did I," said Mrs. Kimmelfarber.

Pop! Pop! Pop! Now they all heard it. The sound of popping filled the infirmary. Little pops and bigger pops and poppity-pop-pops kept popping. Henry looked at his arm and in an instant knew where the noise was coming from. His little brown spots were growing bigger and bigger. They were popping out all over him. No longer the size of freckles, they were as big as the chocolate bits his mother used for making cakes and cookies. He could feel them popping out on his arms and face, could feel them growing under his shirt. In less time than it takes to tell it, Henry Green was covered with little brown lumps from the top of his head to the tip of his toes.

Chapter 5

Calling Dr. Fargo

IN LATER YEARS, Henry couldn't remember who screamed first. All he could recall was that both he and Mrs. Kimmelfarber were yelling their heads off. And that Nurse Molly Farthing was as cool as a cantaloupe.

"Calm down now, both of you," she said. "Mrs. Kimmelfarber, you go and call Mrs. Green on the telephone. Tell her we're taking Henry to the City Hospital."

Mrs. Kimmelfarber didn't move. She just stood there with her mouth open, staring at Henry.

"You scoot now," insisted Nurse Farthing in a stern tone. "Shoosh . . . off with you!

"And you, Henry Green," she said as Mrs. Kimmelfarber left the room, "are coming with me. Let us go. Quietly. Calmly."

She took his hand, and once again, Henry noticed that it felt good and somehow made him feel better. He kept holding her cool hand as they left the school. All the way to the hospital, as the taxi sped along, Henry held fast to the calm steady hand of Nurse Molly Farthing. In fact, it wasn't until he had been checked by two different doctors and was waiting to be examined by the hospital's chief of children's medicine, Dr. Fargo, that he dared to let go.

"What—what? What—what?" said Dr. Fargo as he came bounding into the examining room. He was a small, round man with a bushy white mustache and a confused look on his face. "What have we here, eh?" he asked. "Boy looks like he fell in a mud puddle."

He leaned down so close to Henry's nose that Henry could smell his puffy breath. It smelled like peppermints. "Didn't fall in a mud puddle, did you, lad?"

"No, sir."

"Didn't think so," said Dr. Fargo. "Too bad, would have explained what those big brown spots are all over you."

"Well, then," he said, turning to Nurse Molly Farthing, "tell me things."

"You're not going to believe this, Doctor," Nurse Farthing began, as she told Dr. Fargo about the events of the morning.

"I am not going to believe this," Dr. Fargo repeated when she had finished. "It's impossible. No rash in the whole history of rashes ever appeared so fast. Or grew so big. Or popped out with a noise you could hear. Impossible!"

"It happened," said Nurse Farthing.

"So I see. Well, we'll soon get to the bottom of this or my name's not . . . er. What is my name, by the way?"

"Dr. Fargo, I believe," said Henry.

"Pleased to meet you, son," said Dr. Fargo, and he shook Henry's hand. "Ought to do something about those big brown spots, though."

"Yes, sir," said Henry, who was beginning to feel confused himself.

Dr. Fargo took Henry to the examining table and switched on the big lamp. For a full five minutes he said nothing but "hmmmm" and "hah" as he poked and prodded Henry. He looked at every big brown spot and at all the bare spots in between the brown spots. He looked with a magnifying glass and without a magnifying glass. In Henry's eyes and ears and nose and even under his tongue. Finally he said, "I don't know any more than when I started. They look just like your typical big brown spots . . . except, of course, in the whole history of the civilized world there has never been a case of big brown spots before."

"I'm frightened," said Henry.

"I'm Dr. Fargo," said the doctor, "that much I know. Now what I'd like to do is get to know more about those brown spots of yours." He wet the tip of a cotton swab and brushed it gently against one of the big brown spots on Henry's right arm.

"Ouch," said Henry.

"Did that hurt?"

"No."

"Then why did you say 'ouch'?"

"Because," said Henry, "I *thought* it was going to hurt."

"I see," said Dr. Fargo. Shaking his head, he put the cotton swab into a glass jar. "Take this to the laboratory at once," he said to one of his assistants, and the man rushed out of the room.

"In a few minutes we'll know more about those big brown spots of yours," the doctor said. Hands behind his back, he began to pace the room. Sud-

denly he stopped, his nose in the air. "Who has been eating a candy bar in my office?" he demanded.

No one answered.

Dr. Fargo's nose twitched from side to side as he sniffed the air. "I smell candy," he said. "Someone's been eating a candy bar."

Just then the telephone rang, and Dr. Fargo bounded across the room to answer it. "What— what?" he said into the phone. "Are you sure?" His white mustache bounced up and down as Dr.

Fargo sank slowly into a chair. He put the telephone down, a look of amazement on his face. "Chocolate," he said. "Those big brown spots . . . are pure chocolate. . . ."

"Chocolate?" gasped Nurse Farthing.

"Chocolate?" exclaimed Henry Green.

"Chocolate?" echoed Dr. Fargo's two assistants.

"Exactly," said Dr. Fargo. "The boy, it seems, is nothing more than a walking candy bar!"

Chapter 6

Catch That Boy!

THERE WAS MORE EXCITEMENT than Henry had ever seen. All kinds of doctors were examining him now, poking and prodding as if he were not a boy, but a pincushion. And Dr. Fargo was bounding about the room, talking about "Chocolate Fever" . . . "a new disease" . . . "making medical history" . . . and things like that.

Henry was tired. And afraid.

He wanted to be left alone. He wanted all the doctors to go away. He wanted to be home. He wanted, in fact, to be just about any place in the world except this hospital.

So he did something very simple. Something his heart told him he had to do to survive.

He jumped off the examining table and began to run.

In a flash he had bolted through the doorway and was running down the long corridor. Behind him he heard shouts of "Stop!" and "Catch that boy!"

Two nurses at the end of the corridor tried to catch him, but Henry was simply too quick. He

dodged past them and darted down the stairway. Down, down, down he went, down three whole flights of stairs and out into the main lobby of the hospital. Ahead of him a guard at the door held out an arm. Running as hard as he could, Henry crashed through his grasp and into the street.

Without pausing to think where he was headed, Henry ran. As he was about to turn the corner, he looked back. There was a whole army of people pursuing him. Doctors in white coats, nurses, guards blowing whistles, policemen waving their arms. And behind them he could see Dr. Fargo.

Henry didn't wait to see any more. "Legs," he said, "don't fail me now." And with that he turned the corner and took off down the street.

He ran and ran until he had no breath left. And then he ran some more.

His legs flashing in the afternoon sun, Henry darted down one street and up another. He had no idea of where he was. He had no idea of where he was going. But still he kept running.

People stared at him as he whizzed by. A few even raised their hands, as if to stop him or say something, but Henry kept right on running.

After a long while he couldn't see or hear any of the people running after him. *I must be far ahead of them by now*, Henry thought. But suddenly, up ahead at the corner, a police car flashed by with its siren screaming. *They must be after me*, he thought with alarm. *I'm a wanted man!*

Sick at heart, Henry pushed himself to run faster. His head hurt. His side hurt. His legs hurt. But he kept running.

44

His lungs hurt. His eyes hurt. Even his hair began to hurt. But Henry kept running.

At last he could run no more. He was finished. Done. He had to rest, and to rest he had to hide. Without thinking about it, Henry ran down a large grassy alley that lay between two white houses. At the end of the alley was a large garage with one door partly open. Henry sneaked in and looked around. There was an automobile parked inside, but not a person in sight. With his last bit of strength he flopped down on the floor beside the automobile.

A fine mess you're in now, he thought. *You've run away from a hospital, the police are after you, your mother must be scared to death with worry, and you have a disease no one has ever heard of before.*

The more he thought about his predicament, the sadder Henry became. A lump rose in his throat. A tear ran down his cheek. A sob escaped from his lips. And he was crying, sobbing out loud, really crying.

He cried for a few moments because he was so sad. He cried some more because he was lost. And then he cried for a long, long time because everything had become so hopeless.

At last, when he could cry no more, Henry dried his eyes and tried to think out his situation. He would not go back to Dr. Fargo and the hospital, of that he was certain. Nothing on earth, or any other planet, could make him do that.

But what if he went home? What would his mother and father do?

They would take him back to Dr. Fargo and the hospital. They would have to.

"Never," Henry said aloud, "never, never, never!"

In the dim light of the garage, Henry looked at the big brown spots on his arm and began to hate them. *Stupid spots,* he thought, *why did you have to happen to me?* Feeling angry, he stood up and began to pace the half-empty garage.

I can't go home, he thought, *and I won't go back to the hospital. All right then, I'm on my own. Somewhere there must be a place for me. A place to go until these stupid big brown spots disappear. A place far away, where no one has ever heard of me or the hospital or Dr. Fargo or my parents.*

Feeling much braver now, with things somehow settled in his mind, Henry lay down to rest for a while before setting off on his journey.

Chapter 7

In the Schoolyard

IT WAS ALMOST TWO HOURS later now, and the sun was somewhat lower in the sky. Henry looked cautiously out of the garage, saw no one, and started on his way.

He walked for a long time, trying to stay on side streets and being careful to avoid attention. It was not easy. People kept staring at him. Henry ignored them and kept on walking.

In the middle of the street down which he was walking stood a school. Henry could see lots of boys playing in the schoolyard. He decided to walk through the yard to get to the next street. As he started through, all the boys stopped playing basketball and pitching-in and roller-skate hockey to look at him. It was as if all the noise and action had become frozen, like a movie or a TV show that stops suddenly.

Henry kept going. As he was about halfway through, just about in the middle of the yard, the kids seemed to come to life again. In less time than it takes to tell about it, he was surrounded.

Henry looked around him. All the boys stared back. They had formed a tight circle around him. Henry didn't like it.

One of the tallest boys, who looked a good deal older than Henry, spoke up. "Boy, are you ugly!" he said.

"Yeah," said another boy in the crowd, "really ugly."

"Ugg-*ly!*" echoed another boy.

I'd better be polite, Henry thought. "Excuse me," he said in a quiet voice, "could I get through, please?"

The boys didn't move.

The big boy, who seemed to be a leader, spoke again. "I've seen pimples before, but those are ridiculous."

"They're not pimples," another boy said, "they're warts."

"Yeah, warts," said another, "they gotta be warts."

Now all the boys were speaking up.

"Ugliest warts in the whole world."

"In the world? Man, they are the ugliest warts in the universe!"

"I thought I seen ugly kids before, but this one is out of sight!"

"Horrible!"

"Disgusting!"

"Revolting!"

"And he smells, too," a fat boy with glasses said. "Yuch! Like a stupid candy factory."

"Nauseating!"

The more the boys called him names, the worse Henry felt. He opened his mouth to say something, but nothing came out.

The big boy in the crowd held up his hands to

50

silence the others. "Quiet down, you guys," he said. "I want to talk to Mr. Ugly here."

In a few moments the crowd was silent.

"Now then," the big one said, "you—Mr. Ugly —what's your name, kid?"

Before Henry answered, he thought carefully. He was ashamed of himself and the way he looked. But he was even more ashamed of the gang around him. How dare they act so mean? He hadn't harmed them. And now, when he could certainly use a friend, they had clearly marked him as an enemy.

Henry got angry, but he kept his anger firmly under control.

"My name is my own business," he said. "It's no concern of yours."

The gang hooted and shouted at Henry's reply. A few even whistled.

"Don't be fresh, kid," the big boy said. "We don't like fresh kids here."

A few of the larger boys edged closer to Henry, closing the ring around him tighter.

"Let me hit him, Frankie," a voice said.

51

"Let me get him," another boy said.

Henry thought quickly. "Touch me and you die," he said. "I have a rare and mysterious disease. Whoever touches me will catch it and die a horrible death!"

The gang stopped closing in on Henry.

"Oh, yeah?" said the big boy. "You expect us to believe that?"

"I don't care whether you believe it or not," Henry said.

"You're bluffing."

"Bluffing?" Henry said, "touch me and you'll find out if I'm bluffing. I have Chocolate Fever, one of the most horrible and catching diseases in the world."

"Chocolate Fever?" echoed the big boy. "You're making it up."

Henry could see that he had the crowd on the run. "Chocolate Fever is the worst disease ever discovered on earth," he said. "You know what happens if you get Chocolate Fever? Your whole head swells up. Your mouth gets dry. You break out in big chocolate spots—like me. You begin to

look . . . ugly. And then the really bad stuff begins."

The boys were listening closely now. And the circle around him was beginning to widen as the gang started to back away.

"He's making it up, fellas," Big Boy said. "Don't listen to him." But the boys were listening all right and believing every word. Henry began to walk toward the boys. As he did, they made way for him. Slowly, a path opened, giving him room to get by.

"I don't want you to die," Henry said as he passed through the ring of boys, "so you'd just better let me be on my way."

None of the boys tried to stop him. Even Big Boy, as Henry passed close by, made no move to touch him.

Just as Henry neared the outer ring of boys, he heard one of them exclaim: "Hey! I know who he is. I heard it on the radio when I came home from school. There's a kid who ran away from a hospital this morning . . . and the police are looking for him. His name is Henry Green."

Big Boy called out as Henry kept walking, "Is that you, kid? Are you Henry Green?"

"Henry Green?" Henry called back over his shoulder. "Never heard of him."

Just the same, as soon as he was clear of the schoolyard, Henry broke into a run and didn't stop until he had left the gang far, far behind him.

Chapter 8

Mac

THE TRUCK THUMPED AND RUMBLED along the superhighway, its powerful headlights cutting a yellow slice through the blackness. "Are you all right up there, kid?" the driver called.

From the sleeping bunk set up high in the cab of the big diesel Henry answered, "Right, Mac, I'm okay."

Okay, Henry thought bitterly, *sure I'm okay. I don't have a friend in the world, I look like some sort of side-show freak, the police and doctors and my folks and heaven knows who else is after me, and I don't know where I'm going. If that's being okay, then I'm okay.*

He had stood out on the highway for a long time and watched the day turn into dark. Hundreds of cars and trucks had swept by without stopping. But Mac had stopped and offered him a lift. That was hours ago, and they had come a long way. Henry didn't know how many miles they had traveled or where they were heading, and what's more he didn't care.

He was sure that Mac had not seen his spots. It had probably been too dark to notice them. *No one in his right mind would have anything to do with me,* Henry thought. *Not once they got a look at these stupid big brown spots. Even Mac, nice as he seemed, wouldn't have taken a chance if he had seen me clearly.*

"Hop in," Mac had said, "the weather's fine," a big grin crossing his friendly face. He was a huge black man dressed in dirty coveralls. His truck was clean and warm, and Henry didn't hesitate. After sitting alongside Mac for an hour or so in the front seat, Henry had climbed up to the bunk

and fallen quickly asleep. He didn't know how long he had slept, but he felt rested now.

Mac turned the big truck off the highway and onto a service road. Slowly, he shifted down through the gears and, braking gently, brought the huge trailer to a stop.

"Hey, kid," he called. "Come on down here."

Henry climbed down to sit beside Mac.

"Suppertime," Mac said. "Now just as soon as I get the lights on—"

"I like the dark," Henry said quickly.

"You what?"

"I like the dark," Henry said as the lights came on. Henry blinked at the sudden brightness. *He's seen me now*, he thought.

Mac reached down below his seat and brought up a big picnic basket. He placed it between them on the seat.

"Now let's just see what that woman gave us for supper," he said.

"It's all right," Henry said. "I'll get off here."

"Huh?"

"I won't make any fuss," Henry said. "I'll just go quietly."

"You are a strange one, kid," Mac said. "Now what are you talking about?"

"Well, you must see these big brown spots all over me by now . . ."

Mac nodded. "Yeah, I see them." He began looking through the picnic basket. "You like ham and cheese?"

"I'm willing to go," Henry began.

"Maybe chicken spread? We got chicken spread, too. And I do believe . . . yes, by heavens, tuna fish."

"I mean," Henry began again, "if you don't want to have anything to do with me, I'll understand. I really will."

"What'll it be?" Mac asked. "Tuna, chicken spread, or ham and cheese?" He was looking squarely into Henry's face, smiling ever so slightly.

"Tuna," Henry said after a moment, taking the sandwich Mac handed him.

"Glory be, we eat at last," Mac said.

Henry gobbled the tuna sandwich in nothing flat, then went on to dispose of a ham and cheese, an apple, a piece of raisin cake, and half a thermos bottle of milk.

There was chocolate cake, too, but Henry declined it. Somehow, it didn't appeal to him.

When they had finished eating, Mac settled back and lighted a cigar.

"Mac," Henry said, "isn't there something you want to ask me?"

"Sure, but I figure you're about to tell me what I want to know."

"Well," Henry began, "I have this disease called Chocolate Fever. That's what these big brown spots are all over me—chocolate. And nobody, especially a doctor named Fargo, knows what to do about it. So I'll probably have these spots on me for the rest of my life and—"

"And that's why you're running away," Mac said.

"I have to run away," Henry said. "I look so terrible and ugly."

"I wouldn't say ugly," Mac said. "Unique, maybe."

"What's that?"

"Sort of special."

"But how can I live this way? I'm a freak, a chocolate freak!"

"Easy now," Mac said, "calm down."

"People will be looking . . . staring at me. How can I live with people staring at me?"

Mac chuckled softly. He looked away from Henry.

"How would you like it, Mac, if people stared at you?"

"You know, kid, I've had some experience in that line myself," the big man said quietly.

"You mean people stare at you?"

"Uh-huh," Mac said. "When you're black, and most of the other people are white, that's bound to happen."

"Gee, Mac," Henry said, "I'm sorry."

"Oh, it's nothing personal, kid. Besides, by the time I was your age I'd gotten over it. But you know, getting stared at—and some other things— got me thinking: If there's so many white people, and so few black people, why that kind of makes *me* unique."

"You mean special?"

"Exactly right. So all that staring and stuff, what it did was make me proud. You know, black is beautiful."

"That's okay for you," said Henry, "but white with big brown spots all over is ugly."

Mac put his hand to his mouth and coughed. For a moment, Henry thought he might be laughing.

"Okay, youngster," he said, "have it your own way. Just tell me, where are you going? What you figure on doing?"

"I'm just running away, Mac. And I don't know what I'm going to do."

Mac thought about that for about a second and a half. "Just flat out running away, huh? Things get too much for you, so you cut out? Brilliant."

"I won't go back," Henry said. "I just won't."

"Okay, then, you won't go back. But let me ask you something: You got a mother?"

"Yes."

"Father?"

"Yes."

"They been good to you?"

"Yes."

"Don't beat up on you?"

"Of course not."

"Don't make your life miserable?"

"No."

"So they're pretty good parents, right?"

"Right."

"And you love 'em cause they're so kind and good, right?"

"Yes."

"Well, how do you think they feel right now? Wondering where you could be, are you all right? Are you dead, maybe? Yes, sir, you sure are treating them mean. Why, it wouldn't surprise me if your mother was crying her heart out right now. Just sick to death with worrying about you."

"But, Mac—"

"Now you hush till I'm finished with what I got to say. A good child respects his parents, yes, sir! A good child don't cause his parents heartache or grief or worry. No, sir!"

Henry didn't try to say anything, but he was listening very carefully.

"Now here's *my* plan, kid. First thing we do is

drive down this road till we get to a telephone. Then we call your folks so they can stop worrying."

"I'm not going back to that hospital," Henry said firmly.

"We'll tell that to your folks, too. Maybe there's someplace else you can go . . . some other doctor who can take care of you."

"I like that idea," Henry said.

"Who knows?" Mac continued. "Maybe this chocolate fever of yours will go away. Maybe you'll just wake up tomorrow and it'll all be cured."

"I hope so," said Henry, "but I don't think so."

"Anyway, first thing we do is call your folks. Okay?"

Henry smiled. There was something about the way Mac spoke that made him feel better.

"How about it?" Mac asked. "Should we go find that telephone?"

"What are we waiting for?" Henry said.

Chapter 9

Hijacked

MAC DOUSED THE CAB LIGHTS and reached for the switch that would start the diesel. But at that very moment, a loud voice from the darkness outside the truck called "Reach for the sky! Don't make a move! Hands up! We got you covered!"

Mac froze at the wheel. Henry's heart leaped up in his throat, ricocheted around, and settled back down in his chest again.

Two men jumped up onto the truck, one on each side. Each man carried a small blue revolver. The guns were pointed straight at Mac.

After a moment, Mac found his voice. "What is this?" he asked.

The man on Mac's side of the truck, the one with the mustache, replied. "This, sir, is a robbery. A stickup. A hijacking, in fact. Section Three, Part Four of the Criminal Code. Seizure of a cargo of goods from a vehicle or vessel on the roads or waterways."

"Oh," said Mac.

"Right, Louie," said the man on Henry's side of the truck. He was the smaller of the two thieves, and instead of a mustache, he wore horn-rimmed glasses and a lopsided smile. "I'm Lefty, he's Louie," the man went on. "People get us mixed up sometimes, but I don't know why."

"My name is Henry Green," said Henry, "and he's Mac."

"Pleased to make your acquaintance, I'm sure," said Louie, "even under these unfortunate circumstances." Polite as they seemed to be, Louie and Lefty were still pointing their guns at Mac and Henry.

"You sure you want to do this?" Mac asked slowly. He seemed to be puzzled by the hijackers.

"I think you're going to be in a whole lot of trouble."

"Trouble?" said Louie. "You will be in trouble if you don't do exactly what I say. Now climb up to that bunk up there, both of you, so we can get on with the job."

Henry did as he was told, with Mac following slowly behind him. Mac was getting angry, Henry could see, but when he spoke, his voice was calm. "I don't suppose it would do much good to tell you that you are definitely breaking the law," he said.

Louie laughed. "Breaking the law? Mister, we are fracturing it." And with that, Lefty jumped into the driver's seat, Louie took his place beside him, and the truck began to roll.

Mac still had something on his mind, and above the roar of the motor he called down to the pair of thieves: "You better stop now . . . I think you're making an awful mistake."

"There's no mistake about it," Louie called back over his shoulder. "We know exactly what we're doing. We're hijacking a cargo of expensive furs."

Mac looked dumbfounded at this last piece of news. "Furs?" he cried out. "Furs?" And with that he started to laugh. Great gusts of laughter poured out of Mac, he doubled over one or two times, and, finally, tears came to his eyes and rolled down his cheeks. "Oh, Lord," he cried when he could finally speak, "they think they're stealing furs!"

The more Mac laughed, the more concerned Louie became. He signaled Lefty to stop the truck and, when he had, turned to look up at Mac.

In a low voice he said, "No furs?"

Mac, taking care to keep a straight face, simply answered, "No furs."

"Then what?—" Louie began as Mac interrupted.

"*Candy bars!*" Mac shouted, the laughter beginning again. "Haw-haw . . . candy bars . . ."

"Oh, no!" Louie said.

"Chocolate bars . . . haw-haw . . . with almonds."

"Nuts!" exclaimed Lefty.

"And some without almonds."

"What are we gonna do with a load of chocolate bars, genius?" Lefty demanded of Louie.

"Haw . . . and some with crunch . . . haw . . . and some without crunch."

"Chocolate bars! I can't believe it," Louie mumbled.

"You said this job would be like taking candy from a baby," Lefty said in an angry way, "but . . . chocolate bars?"

"And some with caramel . . . haw-haw . . ."

As Mac continued his roll call of the various kinds of candy the truck carried, the two thieves sat silently in the front seat, staring at each other. It was plain that they were amazed.

After a while, Lefty spoke. "What do we do now?" he asked Louie.

"I don't know," Louie replied, "but I'll think of something. Meanwhile, let's get this truck to the hideout."

"And some of it with peanut butter . . . haw-haw . . . but none of it with furs! Haw-haw!"

With Mac's laughter ringing in their ears, the unhappy thieves looked glumly ahead as the truck rumbled through the night.

71

Chapter 10

Taking a Licking

THEY TRAVELED for a long time.

Lefty was driving very carefully, making sure he kept the big truck within the speed limit. From his perch up in the bunk, Mac was keeping a watchful eye on their route.

Henry tried to keep watch, too, but as the hours flew by, he found himself nodding. He was soon asleep, his head cradled on Mac's chest. As the first streaks of dawn appeared in the eastern sky, the big man was still holding his arms about the boy, cushioning his body from the shocks and jolts of the road.

As the truck shifted gears and slowed, Henry's eyes opened. "Shhh," Mac whispered, a finger held to his lips.

"Where are we?" Henry whispered in turn.

Mac put his mouth almost against Henry's ear before he answered. "Far out in the country," he said, "a long way from nowhere.

"Now when we get where we're going," he continued, "I want you to keep a sharp eye on me. Don't do anything sudden, and don't run. Let's just be very careful, hear?"

Henry nodded.

He would follow Mac's lead and do as he was told. The big man was a person you could trust, especially in a tight spot.

They were traveling along a two-lane road now, with just a few houses set wide apart. Lefty was driving the big truck very slowly, looking right and left at every crossroad.

"Any time, now, we're going to turn off," Mac whispered.

Henry agreed. They must be very close to the thieves' hideout, he thought.

73

Lefty slowed the truck almost to a crawl and turned down a small dirt road. The truck bounced along the narrow track, turning right and left through the trees, and in a few minutes came to a stop in a grove of pines, near a small wooden cabin.

When Lefty had turned off the motor, Louie called up to them. "Gentlemen, we have arrived. Last stop—everybody off."

Lefty and Louie opened the cab doors and stepped down out of the truck. "Easy now, you two," Louie said, as Mac and Henry joined them. "No sudden moves. No funny business. No tricks, right?"

"No tricks," Mac said quietly.

Louie had his gun in his hand again, Henry could see. With the gun pointed squarely at Mac, the thieves led them into the cabin. It had one room, dirty and desolate-looking. A wooden table and chairs stood in one corner, and Louie prodded Mac and Henry in that direction. There were no windows in the cabin and no light, either, until Louie lit a small lantern that hung

from the rafters. Lefty pulled a chair over near
the door and sat there, gun in hand, watching
carefully.

"Well, now," Mac said, "what comes next?"

"What comes next is up to you," Louie said.
"Play it smart, and we leave you here when the
job's over. Give us trouble and. . . . Just don't
give us any trouble."

With that, Louie drew a chair over near Lefty,
and the two of them fell into a quiet conversation.
Lefty was angry, that much was clear. "What do
we do with a load of candy?" they heard him say.
Louie spent most of his energy trying to keep
Lefty calm.

"Looks like our friends over there bought a
pack of trouble," Mac said to Henry. "Instead of
furs, they got something they don't want."

"Haw-haw," said Henry and they both had a
quiet chuckle, followed by several minutes of
quiet giggles. When their mirth had subsided,
Henry asked Mac what was really going to happen.

"I don't know," Mac said, "except for this. If

either one of them tries to put a hand on you, I will personally lay them out flat—gun or no gun. So don't you worry, hear?"

There was a kind of iron in Mac's voice now, and Henry was sure that when the moment came, the big man would be ready for it. Just then, out of the corner of his ear, Henry heard a faint and faraway sound. It could have been a dog barking.

Mac heard it, too, and the two of them sat quietly listening. It was barking, all right, but now there seemed to be two dogs barking. Mac put his hand on Henry's arm. "No noise now," he said, "listen."

The barking got louder, and closer, as the seconds ticked by. Louie and Lefty had heard it too. They stood near the closed door, listening for all they were worth.

You had to be deaf not to hear the chorus of yelps and yowls. It was getting louder and louder with every moment.

"Keep them covered," Louie shouted against the din. "I'm going out to see what's happening."

76

Lefty shuffled over to the corner where Mac and Henry sat, his drawn pistol looking them straight in the eyes. Louie, gun in hand, opened the door and froze on the spot. But only for a split second.

For at that exact moment a big German shepherd came sailing through the doorway and landed on Louie's chest. Louie was knocked flat on his back, his pistol clattered across the floor. Behind the German shepherd came a whole army of yelping, barking dogs, all heading straight for Henry. Airedales, Dobermans, a brown and white collie, several spaniels and setters, and a small French poodle. They were yelping and jumping and barking enough to fill the little cabin with noise and confusion. Lefty was stunned, speechless, absolutely confused by the dog riot that was taking place before him. But Mac knew what he was about. In a flash he pounced on Lefty and took the pistol right out of his hand.

Then he leaped to where Louie's gun had fallen and scooped that one up, too. One gun in each hand, Mac whirled to face the pair of confused crooks. Louie was still on the floor. Lefty was surrounded by a pack of yipping-yapping dogs. Even if he wanted to run, he couldn't.

Henry, of course, was the star attraction for the animal army. They were licking him as if he were some sort of new dog yummy. His arms and legs and face were covered with happy, licking dogs.

And all of it made him laugh so hard he could scarcely protest.

While this was going on, still more dogs were racing into the tiny cabin. And behind them came people—most of them with leashes in their hands—and all with the same puzzling story. They had been out walking with their dogs when, one after the other, the animals had put their noses in the air, sniffed wildly, and then began racing madly

along the dirt road as if following an irresistible scent. Now what could have made those animals behave so strangely? And what about those pistols? What was going on in this cabin, anyway? *Why* did the place smell like a chocolate shop?

It took about an hour, and the arrival of the local police, to sort it all out. Mac had a lot of explaining to do, but when it was over, Louie and Lefty were handcuffed. As they were being led away, Henry heard Lefty mutter, "We go after furs, and we get candy bars. We get to our hideout, and we're invaded by dogs. It's getting so a guy can't make a dishonest living anymore."

"Haw! Haw!" said Mac and Henry together.

As the police car turned out of sight at the end of the treelined dirt road, they were still laughing.

"Come on, kid," said Mac, between chuckles, "we've still got some candy to deliver!"

Chapter 11

At "Sugar" Cane's

His name was Alfred Cane, but his friends called him Sugar. Sugar Cane was the owner of one of the largest candy distributing companies in the East. Chances are, if you've ever bought a candy bar east of the Ohio River, it came from Alfred Cane's warehouse.

It was a very large business.

But Sugar Cane was still interested in every one who worked for him. So when he saw Mac's big rig pull up in the warehouse yard, Mr. Cane was very much relieved.

So was Mac. And Henry. They had made that telephone call to Mrs. Green, you see, and a happy, tearful conversation it was. As soon as Mac dropped off his load of candy, he was going to take Henry home.

Henry liked Mr. Cane the minute he saw him. There was something about the twinkle in his eyes that even his spectacles didn't hide, that made him seem friendly. And with his gray hair and mustache, Mr. Cane looked not a little like Santa Claus.

Henry liked Mr. Cane's office, too. It was warm and cozy. And the walls were lined with shelves containing every single product the big warehouse handled. Imagine seeing every kind of candy bar, cookie, and cake all in one spot. It made you hungry just to be there.

When they had seated themselves and recounted their adventures—laughing quite a bit in the bargain—Mr. Cane leaned forward in his chair and took a long, close look at Henry. "Henry Green," he said, "if it won't offend you, I would like to ask you something about those big brown spots you seem to have all over."

It seemed to Henry that he had explained a million times already, but he went through the story again from beginning to end. Mr. Cane was listening closely, paying keen attention to Henry's every word.

When Henry finished, Mr. Cane spoke. "And so you say that this Dr. Fargo of yours called it Chocolate Fever, eh? Hmmm. I find that terribly interesting."

"I find it just plain terrible," said Henry. "Big brown ugly spots all over . . . looking like a freak . . . people staring at me. And all because of chocolate."

"And all because of chocolate," Mr. Cane echoed. He shook his head once or twice, and a strange look came over his face.

There was a long silence. When Alfred Cane spoke again, it was in a quiet voice. "Henry Green," he said, "let me tell you a story.

"It's about a boy I once knew. A boy like you. Oh, this boy loved chocolate, too, like you once did. Chocolate in the morning? Yes. Morning, noon, and night he ate the magic stuff. And if you think you have invented new ways of chocolatiness, so did this lad. Chocolate-covered fried chicken! Chocolate french toast . . . with chocolate syrup. There was no end to the ways of chocolate with this boy I'm speaking of.

"And, like you, a strange thing happened to him. In fact, the very same thing."

"You mean?" said Henry, suddenly excited.

"Yes," said the old man with a nod, "big brown spots all over."

"Chocolate Fever!" Henry exclaimed.

"The very same."

Henry could hardly contain himself. "But how did he—"

"How was he cured, you mean?" Alfred Cane was smiling now. "Well, the cure was in two parts. And the first was the most important. You see, this boy I once knew had to learn a very sad lesson, as all young people must do. Although life is grand, and pleasure is everywhere, we can't have *everything we want every time we want it*! It's a hard lesson, but it comes in time."

"Yes," said Henry, "I think I understand. Maybe I have had too much of a good thing."

"Indeed."

"I'll eat less chocolate, then. Only when I really, really want to."

"Very good. That is half the battle."

"And the second half?" Henry asked.

Alfred Cane smiled. "Very simple, when you think about it. What is the exact opposite of chocolate? What is the one flavor that is the reverse of the chocolate we know and love?"

"Vanilla!"

Mr. Cane walked slowly to his desk, opened the top right-hand drawer, and brought out a small white box. "Vanilla pills, Henry Green. The very thing that will cure your Chocolate Fever within the hour. That is, if you have truly learned the first—and hardest—part of your cure."

Henry could hardly speak. He wanted to laugh, he was so happy. He wanted to cry, he was so sad. But all he could do was nod.

"Wahoo!" said Mac with a whoop. "Vanilla pills! Who would have thought it?"

"There's one more thing," Mr. Cane said. "That young man I spoke about, the one who reminded me so much of you."

"Yes."

"When he grew up, he decided to spend his life bringing joy and happiness to others. And the way he did it, you see, was to bring chocolate to the world. To make sure that when anyone wanted pleasure, there would be chocolate some-place close by."

Henry thought he knew who that other boy was. "His name?" he asked.

"His name was Alfred Cane," said Alfred Cane, "but his friends called him Sugar." Mr. Cane stepped forward and shook Henry's hand. "Now you run along with Mac. And if you take those pills on the way, I guarantee that your Chocolate Fever will be gone by the time you get home. Good-bye now, and remember what I've said."

"Good-bye, Mr. Cane," said Henry.

"You can call me Sugar."

"And you can call me Henry."

Chapter 12

The Lesson Learned

"HEY, SLEEPYHEAD," said Mrs. Green, shaking Henry's shoulder ever so gently, "are you going to sleep forever?"

Henry stretched and yawned, smiling up at his mother. It was good to be back in his own bed. Good to be where he belonged.

It was Sunday in the Green household. In fact, it was Sunday all over the world. And in the dining room, all the Greens were having a late and lazy breakfast.

"If you can shake - a leg just a little," Mrs.

Green went on, "I think we might manage to have some pancakes ready for you, dear. Just the way you like them."

Henry hopped out of bed. He felt wonderful this morning. The way he always used to feel. He brushed his teeth carefully and paused on his way to the breakfast table only to make a few ugly faces at himself in the mirror. With all those big brown spots gone (forever, he hoped) he didn't look half-bad, except when he crossed his eyes.

There was a big greeting for Henry when he sat down at the table. Elizabeth, who was wearing her special blue dressing gown, even kissed him. And Mark stopped eating long enough to stick out his hand and ruffle Henry's hair.

"There is lots of news for you today, Henry," Daddy Green said as Henry was drinking his orange juice. "The company that makes all those candy bars sent me a letter. They want to give you some kind of award for helping to foil that hijacking."

"Really, Dad?" said Elizabeth. "That's super."

"Yes, indeed," Henry's father went on, "it

surely is. And Mac called just a few minutes ago. Wanted to know if we could go over to his house tomorrow and have dinner with his family."

"Could we, Dad?" asked Henry. "Gee, that's swell."

"Right, son, we certainly can. And Nurse Molly Farthing is dropping by this afternoon, just to say hello, and there's even more news."

"My goodness," said Mrs. Green on her way to the table with Henry's pancakes, "everything seems to happen at once to our Henry. Dr. Fargo wants to see you after school on Monday."

"Do I have to?" said Henry.

"Yes, you have to," Daddy Green said.

"Okay," said Henry, although he didn't like it.

"He's a good doctor, dear," Henry's mother said, "and if you like, I'll go with you.

"Now here's your pancakes," she said as she placed a steaming stack before Henry, "and for a special treat, just this once, I have your favorite chocolate syrup."

Henry's face lit up. His hand shot out and took

hold of the syrup pitcher, but just as he was about to pour the sweet brown mixture over his pancakes, he changed his mind. "You know what, Mom?" he said. "Just this once I think I'll skip it. Plain old maple syrup will do."

The family stared at Henry, as well they might. It was the first time they had ever seen Henry turn away from anything that had to do with chocolate.

His father's smile was as wide as a river. "Enid," he said, "I think our little one is growing up fast."

Henry was into his pancakes now, and they were quickly disappearing. The syrup was good and mapley, the pancakes had a delicious wheat flavor, and washed down with cold milk it was extra good. But still, something was missing. Some taste. Some kind of spark that would make it even better.

There was a small can of cinnamon on the table which Elizabeth sometimes used on her toast. Henry wondered how cinnamon would taste on what was left of his stack of pancakes. He reached

out for the canister and sprinkled just a little bit of cinnamon on his plate. Then he tasted it.

Hmmm, Henry thought, *that's pretty good. In fact, it's very good. I wonder how cinnamon would be on cereal? Like oatmeal, maybe. Or cream of wheat. And maybe cinnamon would be good on other things. Ice cream or French Fries or maybe even . . . cinnamon milk!*

And then Henry had still another thought. *Could you ever have too much cinnamon? Could a person overdo it and . . . was there such a thing as Cinnamon Fever?*

What do you think?